Into the Murky Water

Charles Harvey

Published by Wes Writers and Publishers, 2024.

This is a work of fiction. Similarities to real people, places, or events are entirely coincidental.

INTO THE MURKY WATER

First edition. March 10, 2024.

Copyright © 2024 Charles Harvey.

ISBN: 979-8224643844

Written by Charles Harvey.

Into the Murky Water

by
Charles Harvey

Table of Contents

Dedication

To the innocent ones

"HATE DESTROYS THE HATER... That's a heavy burden to carry."

Wheeler Parker—cousin to Emmett Till

Introduction:

The Fan
What y'all aim to find by
digging up his old bones?
Old old bones, old and innocent bones
Why y'all want to disturb him?
He ain't with his bones.
He down here in the muck with me
and ain't nobody trying to dig my rusty ass up.
His Mama, bless her heart, she got the bones
and that head that looked like a bad cabbage.
Thousands seen it in Chicago. Millions through *Jet*.
Where was my picture? I suffered.
I used to gleam prissy and howl
now mud bugs nest in my teeth.
I kept the good stuff from that boy—his spirit, his soul, his spleen
caressed it out of his naked body
The real Emmett sometimes he runs up the road to Money
gooses that white gal between her legs—boy still gots
that spunk in him.
Then he runs back to me for shelter.
Carolyn wakes up, rubs her thigh
goes back to sleep. 1955 was a long time ago
She wants to rest. I want to rest, and even Emmett.
You got the pictures. You won't forget
Every now and agin some black boy still gets
drug behind a car, still gets strung up in a tree
or the roof rafters of a county jail
They still make fans like me
heavy enough to drown boyish devilment.

INTO THE MURKY WATER

Part one

Alvin in all black leather from head to toe, out of place in the Mississippi heat, gunned his motorcycle. It growled as he and his passenger waited to take off. Jill in blue-jean shorts, white strapless tank top, and pink high-top sneakers hugged his waist. Strands of blond hair fell around her shoulders from underneath her blue helmet. The silver and blue motorcycle had stopped at the corner of MLK and First Street where the "main drag" intersected with the road that led to the river. The sun appeared pale as a magnolia flower behind a bank of rain clouds. Water glistened off the hood of cars, street signs, and the windows of businesses. The light turned green. Alvin lifted the front of the bike and charged ahead on the rear wheel. Jill raised her metallic arm to the sky and whooped like a cowgirl on a spirited horse. They shot ahead of other cars and passed a sheriff's vehicle parked at a Dunkin's Donuts and roared down MLK towards the bridge that led to the Tallahatchie.

"Ain't that some shit?" Clint remarked to his uncle sitting with him in his pickup truck next to the sheriff.

"Two pieces of shit," the man answered. "And that nigger sheriff just let 'em go by."

"Money ain't shit no more," Clint spat.

"Don't worry, Unk. We boys gonna put her back on the map."

"I TOLD ALVIN THE OTHER night when we finished making love, I said, 'Alvin when you leave me, you will make some woman a good husband. I just wish I was the one.'" Jill sighed and looked at Mamie.

"What did he say?" Mamie asked.

"Nothing. Just traced a circle around my navel with his finger and kept his eyes on the television. Sometimes, I think he's mute."

Jill's silver bracelet tinkled against the metal band of her prosthesis as she sipped her coffee. Mamie frowned. She hated the way Jill's Walmart work polo exposed her fake arm. Mamie thought it looked like something that had fallen off a mannequin. She was old school and believed "deformities" should be hidden. Pregnant women showing their baby bumps raised her ire. Such openness seemed unladylike. Women might as well sit gap-legged on a street corner, thought Mamie as she turned and looked out the window. She didn't care much for Jill's "common" talk either. The two women sat inside a McDonald's near the entrance to the Walmart where they worked, Jill in Infants, Mamie in Loss Prevention. They watched the human traffic bustling in and out of the store. Jill's eyes appeared small and far away behind her thick glasses. Mamie's eyes were alert as she scanned the customers leaving the store. She suddenly bumped Jill's knee under the table and nodded at a heavyset woman.

"Square bulge on her stomach. She done stole TV dinners again. Don't know why the manager keeps letting her come back inside the store. If only I were on duty," Mamie nodded toward an obese woman waddling out of the store pushing a baby carriage. Jill focused on a young black man's ass rising over the waistband of a pair of skinny jeans. Her bottom lip trembled. Mamie cleared her throat.

"I see you got your eyes on the prize."

"What?" Jill looked at Mamie as if she was a stranger.

"You watching his behind like you're the man and he's the woman."

"Nothing wrong with looking."

"You sound like my dead husband."

"Well, I ain't dead."

"Naw, you ain't." Mamie sucked her teeth. A young couple pushing a stroller walked past them. "How is your young piece of meat doing?"

Jill looked at Mamie and frowned.

Mamie continued. "Well, he is just a boy and—"

"Who's just a boy?"

"I'm talking about Alvin."

"Oh. And your point is?" Jill raised her brow.

"This thing you have for black men—young ones at that."

"Am I going to have to listen to more of your racist talk?"

"How can you call me racist?"

"Well, you're the one who has a problem with me liking black men. You're the one always bringing up the past."

Mamie looked at Jill's hair. The top of her head zigzagged in a pattern of cornrows that turned into long blond braids that fell over her shoulders.

"People are talking."

"I can't help folks talk. And that 'boy' is eighteen!"

"I know this town. Just because you spent time in New York with that Puerto Rican don't mean you can bring them ways to this place."

"Don't forget I was born here too a few decades after you—thank God. That era you're talking about died up the road. That old store is about to fall down. These are new times. Nobody gives a shit about who I sleep with but you."

"Fool, those old ways ain't dead. You done forgot your daddy?"

"Him and his kind don't count anymore. And men don't give a shit about who's been riding my belly. My stomach could read like the Vietnam War Memorial, and who would give a shit? You know what they ask when they get through fucking me?"

Mamie looked off.

"They ask have I ever had it like that before or was it good. Black and white, it's the same damn question. I've started telling them, 'Yes, I have, darling.' You ought to see the lights go out in their eyes. Men don't give a damn about who's been fucking me. It's all about their ego and dick getting some action."

"But Alvin is so young. Only three years older than..."

"I knew you was going to bring up that Till boy." Jill snatched off her glasses and wiped them across her shirt.

"I was born five years after they killed that child," Mamie continued.

"Look, Mamie, this ain't the old Money Mississippi. Times have changed. Look at all the whites and blacks shopping together and working together in this big ol' Walmart. You a black woman got a better job than me. You can put your handcuffs on black or white shoplifters. You call the cops, and a black Sheriff shows up."

"The more things change, the more they stay the same."

"Ain't nothing the same, but your racist talk. Now finish your Coke, girl. Ain't you got some TV dinners to protect?" Jill laughed and touched Mamie's wrist.

"Girl?" Mamie looked at Jill.

"Oh, I guess I'm being racist now?" Jill winked.

Mamie snatched her hand away and rolled her eyes.

TWO GIRLS STOOD IN front of Hank's Ice Cream on MLK as Alvin drove by. They looked at each other, licked their ice cream and started down the sidewalk toward the Walmart.

"What's wrong with that dude from up north," Crystal asked her friend Shequella.

"I don't know what's wrong with that fool."

"Maybe he's trying to prove something," Crystal flicked her tongue all around the cool white cream.

"How is he gonna prove anything hooking up with that lame ass white trash?"

"I think he's cute," Crystal said.

"You can think what you want. I think he looks like a monkey. And how is running around with trash proving anything? She's cripple, works at Walmart, and she lives in the projects. If he was trying to prove anything, he'd get him one of them Prather girls."

"I thought you didn't like them."

"I don't like their stuck-up asses. I told Beau Jr. if I ever caught him talking to one of them yellow bitches, I'd cut his nuts off. Still, it makes more sense for boys to be talking to one of them girls or any girl but that thing Jill—a cripple white hoe at that."

"I heard she was a hoe. Be giving it up to whoever works at Walmart. I wish I was a hoe."

Shequella looked at Crystal. "Fool what are you talking about?"

"If I was a hoe, I'd be riding on the back of that motorcycle."

"Well go cut your arm off and dye your hair blond. You might have a chance."

ALVIN—BROWN AND LEAN as a deer, slipped through Jill's front door soon after receiving her text message. They liked pretending their affair was secret and forbidden. Of course, the Medgar Evers Housing Project wasn't in the dark. Everyone knew each other's business. Women sucked their teeth as Alvin passed their open windows on his way to Jill's place. Mostly black women and their children inhabited the Evers' barracks-like apartments snaking alongside the shallow bayou that jutted out from the Tallahatchie River. Jill's disability and her low paying job made her eligible for an income-based apartment. She knew by the way her neighbors looked off when she passed by or how they cut their eyes at each other, they didn't like her. When they did speak, she detected veiled hostility when they "complimented" her hair or made mention of her artificial limb.

"You color your hair or is it really blond?"

"You ought to be getting a check with that fake arm of yours. I got both my arms and can't get no job at Walmart."

"Girl, us black women just can't get a man."

"We sure can't, girl."

"These white women is snatching them from us, snatching them right out of the cradle too."

When Alvin started coming around, her neighbors stopped saying anything altogether, letting their silence speak their thoughts. Sometimes Jill spoke to be polite, only to be met with a threatening, *"You talking to me?"*

Once inside Jill's apartment, he took off his black polo shades. Anything black meant cool to him. He wore black like a shield, blending into with the night when he rode or walked along the river.

His chin jutted slightly with a pinhead nick in the center. His dimpled cheeks made him appear more boyish than his eighteen years. He tried to disguise his baby face with sideburns that looked like iron shavings on his smooth caramel face. The girls in Chicago called him a little elf which he hated. He stood in the kitchen of Jill's two-room efficiency listening to the water trickling through the guts of her refrigerator. The tinkling reminded him of her peeing in the toilet after they had made love. He took a deep breath, grabbed his crotch, and stepped into her bedroom. Streaks of moonlight streamed through the loosely drawn blinds and sliced across the bed and floor before disappearing under the bathroom door. Alvin tossed a plastic bag onto the table next to Jill's bed. Cookies a small square white cake, potato chips, canned tuna, and two bottles of beer hit the wooden surface like a hammer and disturbed her pill bottles. She caught her prosthetic arm before it hit the floor.

"If I was dead, you would have woke me up," Jill glared at Alvin and looked at the table. "If you gonna steal out of Walmart, you ought to go for something big like a flat-screen TV."

"Miss Mamie wouldn't let me get away with that." Alvin picked up a beer bottle and twisted off the cap. He held it out to Jill. She pushed herself up against the headboard with her good arm, grabbed the beer, and took a sip. Alvin glanced at the artificial arm and smiled. She shot him an angry look and slid down into the bed.

"Listen, weirdo; we're not going to play that game tonight."

"Aw baby," he pouted. "My back itches."

Jill gazed at him from his head of wild thick hair to his pants hanging like a sack off his hip, down to his white sneakers with the big red shoelaces. She wanted to fuss and make him leave, but he slipped out of his pants and T-shirt and crawled into the narrow bed before she could say another word. Alvin reached for his beer and cinnamon roll.

"Ugh! Cake and beer, what kind of shit is that?" Jill grimaced as Alvin licked his fingers.

"It's not cake. It's a cinnamon roll, and I'm going to give you some." Alvin broke off a piece.

"No, you're not." She turned her head.

With one hand Alvin grabbed Jill's head and with his other hand, he mashed the gooey roll against her lips.

"Ugh, you bastard," she screamed and squirmed to get up. Alvin held her down and looked at her—lips smeared with icing and panting. He leaned forward and they kissed—creamy lips meeting creamy lips. They stopped only to breathe and let Jill pull her nightshirt to her chin. Alvin smiled at the sight of her breasts, stuck his fingers in the icing, and smeared her nipples. Jill lay with her hand across her forehead, fingers cupped as if she was catching raindrops. She felt his manhood through his thin boxers pressing against her thigh. In a moment the sheet and his underwear were tangled around Alvin's ankles. Her heels met across his back. They kissed again before she pushed him gently and nodded toward the night table. He huffed, reached over, and pulled a condom out of the drawer. As she and Alvin cradled each other, Jill closed her eyes and thought about her first time with boys.

She had started middle school with a terrible case of acne. Her grandmother made a concoction with vinegar and fine sugar to use as a face scrub. Smelling like a jar of pickles was not the worse of bad things to happen that year. She discovered sex and how that helped her get on the good side of boys to keep them from teasing her. She knew from looking at Alvin's new driver's license he had been born in 1997, during her year of vinegar and boys. She imagined Alvin slipping out of his mother's womb at the exact moment she sat in the back row of Algebra One letting Sam Gordon run his hand up her thigh. She felt a twinge of guilt over his age and tried to push Alvin off. He sensed something was wrong, eased down her belly and planted a sugary kiss between her legs. Jill seized a handful of his hair and pulled him close.

"I'm glad we have the Internet these days. A dude don't need to take sex education," Alvin said taking a swig from his beer. "I'm really a natural when it comes to making love, but it don't hurt to learn new shit. Right, baby?"

Jill turned over and put her fingers to his lips. He sucked them gently. An hour later, she ushered him toward the door and out into the darkness. He gave her ass a hard squeeze. She instinctively slapped at his arm, but he darted away toward the bayou.

AS ALVIN WALKED ALONG the Tallahatchie, he felt wise and blessed. Chicago and everything ugly in Chicago were seven hundred miles away. Money Mississippi turned out to be a cool place, unlike the image of a backwater town full of confederate flag waving tobacco-chewing rednecks his mother had warned him about. Stepping off the bus at the Money depot, he took in the willows and pines dancing in the breeze. A sense of ease washed over him, as if the trees' limbs were yielding to the street-smart sharpness he carried. His grandfather fed him a healthy diet of steak and greens, plus all of the advice he had in his seventy-year-old head about women and blues. He let the John Lee Hooker, BB King, Charles Johnson, Lead Belly, Muddy Waters, and Son House seep into his soul as he ate. But it was his grandfather's take on women that intrigued him. The old man seesawed between love and disdain. White women raised his ire the most. Anything the old man said not to touch, he had to touch.

He would allow the girls to cast their spell first of course. His grandfather had said that was the gentlemanly thing to do. He loved the spells of white girls and boys—the eyes that changed from blue to green from amber to black at the whim of the sun and moon. There were plenty of girls in Money for Alvin to choose from—ten times more than there was in nineteen-fifty-five when Emmett Till was accused of crossing the color line and met his death. Money had grown on both sides of the Tallahatchie when the Government decided to build a giant warehouse complex at the intersection of the river and the old Yazoo and Mississippi Valley Railroad. The warehouses full of Government surplus built atop a mysterious bunker revived Money and the surrounding towns. The local Walmart store and distribution center brought paved streets and a strip center anchored on opposite ends by Starbucks and Dairy Queen.

"Money has risen from the mud and buried its ugly past," the mayor declared at the ribbon cutting ceremony for Walmart.

Alvin's grandfather wasn't so sure about the past being buried. He was a little boy a few years older than Mamie when he stood next to his father and watched the white men pull Emmett's foul-smelling body from the murky waters.

"Right here is where they drowned that Till Boy. They took him out of his uncle's house to beat him and then they drowned him." Alvin's grandfather pointed to a cross riddled with bullets next to the river. Alvin's Kawasaki was parked nearby.

Alvin replied to a topless photo text Jill had sent him. A lollipop was stuck in her mouth. *"I could be doing this to your lollipop right now,"* the accompanying text read.

"Stop playing with that phone and listen to me," Silas demanded.

"Paw Pee, that's ancient history. Kewane who plays basketball got two white girls."

"Kewane is not my responsibility. You are. Here you are full of Chicago sass and brass dating that old crazy white woman. Why don't you get a black girl your own age? A good-looking boy like you messing with that old cripple woman."

"She's not that old, Paw Pee."

"She's almost old enough to be your mama. You need a black girl young like you. One of the Prather girls. Good looking gals all of them..."

"I'm just spreading my love around, Paw Pee."

"You better watch yourself. That's all I gotta say. That woman's grandpa was a grand dragon."

"Well, all he can do now is belch hot air in hell."

"Enough with that cussin.'

"I'm sorry, PawPee. But everything is *Used to be.* You used to be in Civil rights. Now you're not."

"Fool, just because white folks ain't wearing sheets and we're not marching, don't mean anything has changed. If shit was all right in the world, wouldn't be no need for Black Lives Matter. Which is something you ought to be paying attention to."

"I see plenty of white girls marching with the bros."

"That's not what it's all about. But just remember, what was in Jill's grandpapa ain't dead. A whole lot of shit's done replaced the KKK. Money may be built up, but there's plenty of woods around to bury black bodies."

Alvin opened his overshirt to reveal a BLM t-shirt.

"All right boy, make light of this world at your own peril. Maybe if your daddy was living, he could straighten you out."

"He's gone Paw Pee. Your civil rights didn't save him from a cop's bullet."

"We brought out the truth about his killing. The cops tried to hide behind a lie."

"What does the truth do for a dead black man? Nothing."

"The truth can save your life, boy."

"Yeah okay, Paw Pee. Well, at least Jill is a female."

Silas studied the cross sitting crooked in the mud as if he was counting the bullet holes. He turned and looked at Alvin. "Mae sent you down here to get away from them gangs. I don't believe any of that other stuff she was talking about. But if it is true, messing around with that white woman ain't proving nothing, except you're a fool. Now the Bible says..."

Alvin cut his grandfather off in mid-sentence, with a laugh and kiss on the forehead. He hopped on his bike. Silas watched him ride away. His mother had sent her son to Money to save the boy from one devil, but had he given him another demon that could destroy him? He thought the silver and black chopper would take Alvin toward manhood.

"It's Mississippi. Plenty of backroads. He won't get hurt," he had reassured his daughter over the phone.

WORKING AT WALMART and away from the watchful gaze of his grandfather, Alvin was free to explore a rainbow of experiences. The girls noticed his thick lips and high cheekbones. He let them play in his hair. They nicknamed him "Model Boy." Sometimes dudes stared at him as he walked, paying attention to the way he carried his mother's hips. He used his looks to unlock folded arms and crossed legs. He entered barriers quietly and quickly behind pallets of toilet paper, candy, motor oil, detergents, and scented candles.

Jill was a different kind of challenge for Alvin. At first, he paid no attention to the white woman with the "fake arm" who stared him up and down. He felt slightly annoyed when his co-workers teased him and dared him to "holla" at her.

"I thought you was a Chicago boy. You scared of the one-armed bandit?" Howls of laughter followed the derisive comments.

"I ain't scared of shit."

"Well holla at her then, nigga."

And he did speak. The idea of an older woman intrigued him. He needed to show those Mississippi boys a thing or two. Jill's hard plastic arm with the metallic fingers tugged at his imagination. Rather than being repulsed, he was curious about other parts of her body. He wondered what it would be like to fuck her. His male co-workers laughed at him when he mentioned wanting to screw the woman with the fake arm.

"Aw man, you like that mechanical pussy. I didn't know you was going to take it that far. We just wanted to see if you would holla. You a freak, dude. You a freak in a lot of ways."

The tattoos on each side of her neck shaped like crosses and the braided hair gave Jill a soulful aura. Yes, girls were easy for him. But Alvin found them dull and afraid to try new things. A woman would be more open, and experienced Alvin reasoned. They could teach him a thing or two and let him experiment with things he saw on the Internet. Yes, he was a freak, and she was going to be his cyborg chick.

Alvin's grandfather's admonishment. *"Her granddaddy is a Klu Klucker. Ain't nothing but white trash,"* made him even more curious.

"Forbidden fruit gots the sweetest juice on the vine, and I ain't lyin!"

Alvin thought about that line from the Blues singer Sonny House. Jill became forbidden fruit for Alvin to pull apart and devour like a mad man. He performed his acts fueled by the porn he had watched on the Internet. But like anyone who eats too much, his belly ached from to time. His grandfather made sure old magazines and articles about Emmett Till's murder were sprinkled around the house. Alvin began to seesaw between lust and malice.

"Why are you so quiet tonight?"

"I'm thinking."

"What could possibly be inside that head of yours?"

"Oh, a nigger ain't supposed to think?"

"You can think while I suck your cock."

"You disgust me. All white people disgust me. I bet your grandaddy helped kill Emmett Till."

"You ain't gotta be here drowning in this hateful rage. You can go now."

"I can't go and I can't stay. I wish everyone would leave me alone."

Alvin and Jill went back and forth until he either stormed out of her house or she squatted between his legs.

A woman will make you hate you love her,
and you gonna love her until they throw cold cold dirt
in your poor pitiful face!"

Sometimes on his way home from Jill's he stopped and stared into the Tallahatchie's its murky waters. The moonlight played tricks. Animals scurried through the vegetation. A log resembled a body—moss hanks of hair. The water's stench mingled with the scent of magnolias. A thing plopped into the water. Footsteps crackled behind him. Alvin looked around and made out a tall slim figure coming toward him.

"I threw the rock. I ain't wanted to scare you."

He recognized Clem's slow drawl. Clem worked in Automotive. A whiff of motor oil cut through the air. They stood next to each other.

"They killed that boy a few yards up yonder."

"My granddaddy showed me the other day."

"We heard he saw the body."

"Yeah, he said he did."

"You ain't scared to be out here?"

"Nah, I ain't scared."

"Me either. I ain't scared of nothing but a big mouth." He gazed at Alvin. Alvin looked at him and looked off toward his bike glimmering under the moonlight. At times the water caught the reflection of the wheel spokes.

"That's a nice motorcycle. Real pretty."

"It's okay for something used."

"Don't knock it. Nothing wrong with being pretty. And you real attractive for a dude."

"You too."

"Aw, everybody says I'm too black. Even my mama say so."

"Nothing wrong with being black."

Clem thought about what Alvin said for a moment and laughed. "You don't think so?"

"Nah, man."

Off in the distance, a car blasting rap music pulled into the Medgar Evers. Both Clem and Alvin looked toward the direction of the projects. The music stopped after a moment and all was quiet again.

"What about that white chick you be messing around with?" Clem looked at Alvin.

"What about her?"

"She be all on your motorcycle and stuff."

"So, what about her?" Alvin and Clem stood close to one another. A sweet aroma of cologne from Clem's chest cut through the oil smell.

"I don't know. I know you be watchin' me and shit like that when we be in the bathroom."

"We not in the bathroom now," Alvin said.

"Nah we ain't."

Clem and Alvin locked in an embrace.

JILL HAD HER OWN REASON to keep herself latched to Alvin. She had been poor all of her life. But she had also been watching Alvin and saw in him a chance to taste life on the other side of the railroad tracks. Money had done not only an economic flip-flop but also a cultural one. Alvin lived with his grandfather in a little enclave called Green Mound or "Black Money." BMW's, Jags, and Range Rovers sat parked in the winding driveways. It was a mystery why a group of retired army folks decided that Money Mississippi would make a nice retirement community. Perhaps it was due to the cheap land where poke salad had taken over the cotton and where a parcel of land next to the ugly brown Tallahatchie River could be bought for fifteen cents a square foot in the sixties. For years after the murder, you couldn't give a piece of land away. But Black people (workers from the space center in Huntsville) came and developed the area a two miles from the crumbling Bryant's Grocers. They built sprawling homes with docks for their boats. Named the streets after Chicago landmarks—State Street, Mercantile, and Lakeshore. They erected a memorial to Emmett. However, they shopped and sent their kids to private schools in Jackson. Sociologists called it an act of mass defiance—a thumbing of the nose at the establishment.

"DO YOU KNOW WHY I LIKE having my nipples sucked?" Jill blurted out to Mamie as they sat at a picnic table reserved for smokers.

Mamie looked at her from over the top of her glasses. "Did you forget to take your pills this morning? Asking me some question like that. I don't know, and I'm sure I don't want to know."

Jill continued as if Mamie was all ears. "Because it feels so damn good."

"One of them pills this morning would make you feel even better."

"I don't need medicine. I got love. I got power in these jugs."

"I'm a Christian woman and don't care to hear all your nonsense. You need to be keeping a better eye on your department. Somebody is walking off with a lot of Pampers."

"I've been stealing 'em. The baby is coming."

"Fool, what baby? You told me your daddy had your tubes tied."

"One Doctor can do, and another Doctor can undo."

"Woman, I don't have time for your crazy talk this evening."

"Oh Mamie, I bet you ain't always been a Christian. You know these things got the power." Jill Pointed at her breasts.

"What power you talkin' about?"

"A woman's tits got the power to reduce a man, strip the muscle from his flesh. I don't care how big of a brute he is, you get him to working on your nipples you become his mother of God."

Mamie took a sip of her coke and looked at Jill. She paid close attention to her eyes to see if they were darting and flickering like far away lanterns. The last time Jill had that look it took three Walmart employees and two cops to wrestle her onto a stretcher for a trip to the Jackson State Insane Asylum. Today Jill's eyes were as focused as lasers.

"Ain't that boy too young to be your brute?"

Jill cut those lasers at Mamie. "Why do you keep saying I'm too old for him?"

"Too old and too white. You know the kind of man your daddy is."

"My daddy ain't a man. He's a warthog."

"Whatever he is, he don't like us black folk."

"Alvin is my shield against my daddy."

"You using that boy to make a point to your daddy? You'll get Alvin killed."

"Times have changed, I keep telling you. Money has changed."

"The more things change..."

"I like his quiet innocence," Jill cut Mamie off. "That's what drew me to him."

"I don't think he's all boy. I told you I saw him grabbing on another boy's ass when they was coming out the restroom the other day."

"Aw, Mamie, they were just horsing around. Guys horsed around in the army when they got bore. They weren't gay and Alvin ain't either."

"You don't know what he is."

"You don't like him because he lives in *Black Money*."

"What I care about them high sididitty folks? Just because they all army folks or retired from that space center in Huntsville Alabama don't mean nothing to me."

"Jealous, jealous, jealous," Jill teased Mamie.

"Shut up before I forget I'm a Christian."

"Well, whatever you think of Alvin, don't matter to me. He's quiet fire in my bosom. I know that."

"He's lighting your fire with a big piece of kindling wood. That's what you're after. All you white women want is..." Mamie bit her knuckle to keep from saying more.

"You got too much of the past in you, Mamie."

"I seen the pictures of that thing they pulled out of the river. It wasn't human no more. It was a thing all because of a woman like you."

"Ah nah, honey. If Carolyn had been a woman like me, she'd took that Till boy in the back of that store and made him prove his mannishness."

"Let that child alone. You're over thirty years old, Jill. He just turned eighteen."

"Alvin is my refuge."

"Them pills you take is your refuge. Not some boy."

"It's unnerving how he can look at you like he's drinking you with his eyes. There's nothing vulgar in his gaze. It's all calm like the river on a quiet summer day."

"Rivers do rage from time to time."

"Not my Alvin."

"I'm not talking about Alvin. I'm talking about your daddy."

"That peckerwood klu klucker can't do nothing but huff and puff."

Mamie said nothing. A car parked in front of them and a man got out wearing a T-shirt and jeans patched with confederate flags. He spat a wad of snuff on the sidewalk and continued into the store. A mess of tangled black hair fell over his shoulders. Mamie stood up and looked at Jill.

"Something bad is going to happen again one day around here. I don't know what, but whatever it is, it's going to be an evil thing."

She left Jill staring off into the distance.

ALVIN AND JILL WRESTLED on her cot littered with dingy stuffed animals and a gold foil condom wrapper. They wavered between tension and release, tightness and looseness. Their bodies pulsed from taser-like shocks. When their senses dulled and fatigue threatened to overtake them, they gulped Red Bull and started up again. After a moment, Alvin tensed, gripped Jill's waist, and let out his breath in a long *hmm*.

Perplexed and satisfied, he rolled off her, and they lay quietly listening to each other's heartbeat. The soft drum duets seemed to come from a faraway place. Alvin sat up and looked out the window before falling asleep. A hint of blue covered the sky giving the moon a blue sheen tinting the pill bottles on Jill's dresser. The psych Doctor at the VA in Biloxi had told her to take two pills when it starts to feel like bullets exploding in her head.

"Will it feel like the Fourth of July?" she asked.

In the quiet blue room with Alvin lying motionless beside her snoring, Jill suddenly felt lonely. She remembered her grandmother walking in the woods around their trailer before she died. People often told Jill she was the spitting image of Ruby Godine. As a child, she couldn't imagine the comparison. All she saw was a silver-haired old woman with a neck jutting vulture-like from bent shoulders. But this morning Jill noticed in the mirror on the bedroom door, her grandmother's beak nose, and long chin. She wondered if she would die from breast cancer like the old lady. Jill squeezed her breast and grew fearful she would die childless. The premonition made her quake. She had known a hard, bitter road and had just turned thirty-one. Her bouts of loneliness shattered and broke her like ice falling from branches of a tree. Before and after her stint in the army, all of the arms that had held her turned to ice, and the lips that had kissed hers spewed cold empty promises. She felt doomed.

Jill looked at Alvin. She watched him bat away an imaginary thing from his crotch. She bent over him and caressed his forehead. Her right breast rested against his cheek. She woke him with a kiss on the forehead. He smiled and pulled her nipple into his mouth. She didn't mention the condom. He grabbed her around the waist and plunged between her legs. Jill wet his face with kisses.

"Thank you, God. Thank you for giving me someone I can hold forever," she whispered.

ALVIN'S ANNOUNCEMENT was somewhat of a shock, but not unexpected. He would be off to Morehouse College in the fall. Silas had pushed the idea hard. To him, Morehouse with its history of striving black males would be the cure of what ailed Alvin—that crazy trashy white woman who was leading his grandson astray. Plus, Morehouse was close to Spellman, and he might find him a nice Black girl to marry. He used a brand-new Mustang as bait to get Alvin to sign the college papers. Jill would be an afterthought in a few weeks, Silas reasoned.

Jill shrugged and rubbed her stomach when Alvin told her the news. She looked at the poster of the Flat Iron Building on the wall. All of the men she had known became bearers of bad news. She had erupted when Juan called her a freak and put her out of his apartment. She sneaked back in and destroyed all of his photographs including the negatives. She had done everything he wanted her to do, including working as a stripper in a bar. Her act was the *Mechanical Lady* where she took off her arm and played with herself to the amusement of men who sniffed the fingers of the device. She did all of that to keep her and Juan fed and keep him suppled with cameras and film. And what thanks did she get?

"I DON'T SEE WHAT YOU want with him. He's just a high school boy, and on top of that, he's a nigger. I hope to hell you haven't forgotten what the Marines taught you in hand-to-hand combat training. Aim your finger for the base of his neck and don't miss no chance to kick his balls off. You need to remember that. You're dealing with a savage here."

Roy stood wide-legged glowering at his daughter. What was left of his crew-cut brushed past his ears and scattered across the back of his head like rows of needles. He was dressed in camouflage pants and a T-shirt. On the front of his shirt, Mickey Mouse straddled a rocket aimed at a map of Iran. Underneath Mickey, the caption read "Nukey Mouse." He continued his assault on Jill.

"He looks like a goddamn ape. What if he knocks you up?"

"I love him, daddy."

"You love him? Thank God your Mama and Grandma is dead and can't hear you say that."

"I need him."

"You need. You need." He advanced toward Jill. "Now there's where you and your Mama were alike. She was always needing something—a stray dog or a stray cat. I don't know which is worse, pining after some goddamn nigger or a stray possum."

Jill watched a roach run through the gauntlet of pill bottles on her table, make a flying leap to the floor, and take off running. She wished she could handle pain that way, fly, land on her feet, and take off running.

"Well hell," Roy continued. "Mix it up with that nigger. But don't expect me to be bouncing any black bastard on my knee. Believe that!"

"You don't think I'd have a baby just to bring us closer, do you?"

"No, I don't think that at all. You don't have sense enough to plot a goddamn thing."

Roy turned and looked out the window at the Walmart sign just over the trees on the other side of the river.

"Do his folks know about you?"

"It's just him and his grandfather here in Money. He's going to send him away to Morehouse this fall."

"Who is his grandpa?"

"Silas Brown."

"Uppity nigger."

"I hope he doesn't go," Jill said turning away from Roy.

"Did you ask him to stay?

"Yes."

"What did he say?"

"Just shrugged his shoulders."

"Come September, he'll be gone."

"He'll still be close to me."

Roy turned and looked at Jill. "You realize how far Atlanta is from here?"

Jill smiled. Roy turned and looked at the array of pills on the table.

"Those pills got you addle-brained."

"The Marine Corps was your idea."

"I'm ain't the reason you couldn't cope in there. I didn't tell you to wrestle half the goddamn corps between your legs. I wanted you to be tough, so men wouldn't push you around. You the one who decided to be Snow White and sleep with the Seven Dwarfs—pulling a train with all them niggers. You was the one who disobeyed orders and picked up that IED. Then you go running up to New York behind some nigger who nearly beats you to death."

"He was Puerto-Rican."

Roy looked at Jill. "You're a lost cause living in a zoo around all of these niggers. But shit..." His voice trailed off as he sighed. He sat down on the couch, wrote out a check for her rent, and tossed it on top of the pill bottles. The echo of the slammed door rang in Jill's ears long after her father had left. She sat on the couch staring at his check. In a moment, she touched her stomach and closed her eyes. She tried to imagine pleasant things—flowers, moonlight reflecting off Alvin's wet body as he emerged from a swim in the river. However, her mind floated all over, only to land on her arm lying three feet from her. She had reached down to pick up a purse with money spilling out. She had been warned to stay away from anything that looked suspicious. She convince the medic to let her keep the bone fragment from her mangled hand—a piece of the finger where she would have worn a wedding ring.

Part Two

The baby, curly-haired and so pale he looked bloodless was born on the first day of April. Roy called him an April Fool's joke. Jill named him Ajay combining the first letters of her sand Alvin's names. Three days later, Jill and Ajay stepped into a coin-operated picture-taking booth near Walmart's main entrance. She moved the blanket from his wrinkled face and held him close to her chin. After the near-blinding flash, a strip of four wallet-sized photos dropped behind a glass window. She winced at how startled and vulnerable she looked. Ajay's face looked more like a kitten's than a human's.

At home, Jill placed the photos side by side on the table. As Ajay slept on the couch, she thought about the art gallery where her New York boyfriend had had an exhibit. She imagined her and Ajay's photos blown up as large as picture windows swinging from chains attached to the ceiling. "*Lonely WoeMan With Child*," A plaque proclaimed. Patrons of the gallery drifted through the placards noting and marveling at the tiny details—her stark eyes, the small ducks on Ajay's knitted cap, the way his left hand curled as if squeezing a tiny scepter, her hair looking like a mop of black strings. As Jill daydreamed overwhelming loneliness took over her. Suddenly she was alone in the world with a baby and a mountain of pills.

A day later, Jill wrote Alvin a note on a piece of stationery framed in roses.

"I am a mother. I love you and your son. Come home."

She waited. Three weeks later she mailed another letter and picture to Morehouse College. She waited. Her third missive was full of rage and poisonous words. Jill called Alvin a son-of-a-bitch, screamed and cursed as if he could hear her words. She waited for an answer. Days turned into weeks. Weeks turned into months. Soon she stopped counting, wrapped the remaining small photo in the stationery, and threw it in a drawer. Jill hoped when Ajay saw it years later, he would see the loneliness in his mother's eyes, and perhaps he would never mistreat a woman.

TWO-YEAR-OLD AJAY REACHED into his diaper and grabbed a handful of feces. He ran screaming toward the wall and smeared shit next to Mamie's chair. She jumped up.

"My God, Jill, look at him. How can you stand this? Look, he's got his hand in his mouth! Can't you stop him?"

"Why?" Jill yawned and looked at Mamie.

"What do you mean, why?" Mamie pointed to the wall. "That boy is too big for that. Why ain't you trying to civilize him?"

"He's only two. He's as civilized as he needs to be."

"I can't believe something like that came from a bright boy like Alvin. You sure Alvin is his daddy?" Mamie squinted at Ajay who stood bent over with his head between his knees.

"The last time me and Alvin made love I held on tight to him and felt all of his love pour into me. He said he loved me. He said he wouldn't go to Morehouse. He'd go to Jackson State instead. But I knew he was lying."

"Money done come a mighty long way, but still there ain't enough here to keep a boy like Alvin."

"And certainly not beside a poor white trash girl."

"I didn't say all of that." Mamie cut her eyes at Jill.

"You didn't have to."

"Does Silas come see his grandchild?"

"No. When I called and told him I had had Alvin's baby, Silas acted like he didn't know who I was and hung up. He knows me. Whenever he sees me in Walmart, he turns his head."

"The next time I'm off on Sunday, I'm going to the church he goes and speak to him," Mamie said frowning at Ajay prancing around with his soiled diaper on his head.

"Don't bother," Jill murmured.

"It ain't a bother. That boy favors Alvin. Got his long legs and high cheekbones. You should have left him on Silas' doorstep."

"What kind of Mother abandons her child?"

"Plenty do. Remember that epidemic we had two years ago? I found three babies in Walmart's restroom that year. Them Mexican men were working on more than the highway that year. White women and black women got them some Latin flavor. I'm surprised you didn't."

"I don't like Mexicans." Jill rolled her eyes at Mamie and looked out the window.

ALVIN WOKE UP SWEATY and hot from a recurring dream. For the past few months, the vision had become a fixture. The scenes varied, but the image of a child's amputated foot was a constant theme. At times he walked near a trash dumpster, a body of water, or a field and there would be a child's foot covered with maggots. Once he dreamed, he was taking a shower and looked down, and a foot lay near the drain in the middle of a red swirl of water.

He looked out the window. A gray dawn fog hid the world. Cold New York air seeped into the room where Bruce his fiancé had left the window ajar. Alvin shut it tight and watched Bruce kick off the blanket in his sleep. Alvin crawled back into bed. He felt horny but knew not to wake Bruce—at least not directly. He flipped on the TV and figured the light would wake him and they might kiss and go further. However, Bruce grunted, threw an arm over his eyes, and snored. Alvin sighed and flipped channels aimlessly. He paused at a program chronicling the rise of the New Klu Klux Klan and the political climate that welcomed them. They marched around in Greenwood Mississippi in their khakis and red shirts, looking more like Target employees waving flags than anything menacing. Until now, Alvin hadn't thought much about the summer he spent in Money Mississippi and the white woman he used to screw. There was one jarring phone call from Clem when he was a sophomore.

"Man, what you mean I'm a daddy."

"That one-armed white woman Jill you was fucking is telling everybody her baby belong to you."

"Aw man, that bitch is crazy. Every time I fucked her, I used a condom. Must be somebody else's baby."

"She brought him to the store the other day. He some nigga's baby, that's for sure with that butterscotch color. Mamie say he look like you."

"Do he?"

"I don't know man. He just look like a baby to me. But he got a black daddy, for sure."

"Paw Pee ain't said nothing to me about no baby."

"You know your grandpa treated her with a long-handled spoon. She can't say nothing to him."

"So, man," Alvin changed the subject. *"What you doing with yourself at Walmart?"*

"I'm the Assistant Manager Automotive and Hunting. I got me a little side hustle selling hunting pistols. You want one?"

"Nah man, I'm good."

"I don't know man; niggas don't play up there in the ATL."

"I keep away from trouble."

"Yeah, I imagine so." There was a long pause. Alvin wondered if Clem had hung up. *"I sure miss them rides we used to take on these backroads."*

Alvin was silent.

Well, I guess you got you a college friend now—all them dudes up there in Morehouse. You take care.

Alvin bought a new phone soon after that conversation with Clem and got a new number. To Keep Alvin away from Money, Silas traveled to Chicago during the holidays and spent most of the summer up there. Morehouse and Spellman kept Alvin busy, and he soon forgot Jill, her prosthetic arm, and those nights he spent with her in the Medgar Evers projects.

He hadn't bothered to trouble Bruce with the rumor of him being a daddy, but the TV program brought back memories as he lay in bed, watching red-faced white men waving confederate flags and chanting against race mixing and *"mongrelization."* He slipped out of bed and using the light from the television, fished in a hidden compartment of his old backpack for a bundle of letters. He opened one letter and stared at the child in the arms of a wild-eyed white woman. The boy would be much older than the baby pictured in the photo. Alvin counted in his head. "Five years old," he said to himself. Another letter contained Jill's scrawled notes cursing him and calling his child a bastard. "Daddy?" Alvin said with a big question mark. He remembered either buying or stealing condoms from Walmart. Jill had insisted they use one every time they had sex. But what about the last time or next to the last time. He remembered thinking Jill had slipped up, but Clem had told him Jill was too old to get a baby.

"Daddy," Alvin said to himself. He looked at Bruce still sleeping and smiled. He loved him. He knew that with all of his heart. But two men didn't make babies. They had talked about a plan to each father a child using the same surrogate mother. There was someone they knew and could trust who would go along with the plan. But then Bruce found out he was sterile. It would be one-sided They both wanted the same woman to bear their blood. What were their options? Adoptions? Foster care? But he was a daddy. And if Bruce loved him, he would love Ajay. He just had to.

"WHAT'S THAT TERROR done now to have you so worked up? Mamie nodded toward Ajay who lay sleeping on the couch.

"He's not why I'm crying, this is." Jill thrust a letter toward Mamie.

"What is it," Mamie asked as she took the half sheet of yellow tablet paper.

"A letter from Ajay's great-grandfather."

Mamie's face froze as she read the missive:

"*Alvin is going to soon marry a nice black girl. He ain't ever coming back to Money. And don't you and that bastard go smelling around them. She's a nice girl and I hope they will start them a family soon. I want real Grandkids. Not no illegitimate ones. I understand you been kind of struggling since your pa died. Plus you done lost your job and all. Just write me back on who I need to pay your rent to, and I'll continue making the payments. But don't contact me otherwise.*

Regards."

Mamie gave the letter back to Jill.

"No wonder that boy is so bad," she said looking around the room at the cut-up furniture and the lamp with the zigzag crack running up its side. Look whose blood he got running in his veins.

"Horseshit," Jill said. Alvin ain't marrying no woman. I got this letter from him." She handed Mamie a piece of thick blue stationary with faint lines like graph paper. Mamie read and suddenly stopped.

"What! A man? He's bringing his man friend. To Money?"

"Stop acting so surprised. You said so yourself you saw him feel on a guy's ass when they came out of the bathroom one time. Yeah. He said he and his fiancé are driving to Money to see if I would let them take Ajay for a little while."

"Well honey maybe that's a good idea until you get yourself back together. But I don't know about two men."

Jill laughed. "It'll be three men."

"HOW THAT WHITE COCK feel to you?"

"Clint, is that all I am to you?"

"Hell no, baby. You're my gal. Ain't I gave you a ring?"

Jill peered in the mirror at the tiny diamond ring around her neck and smiled. "There's a big difference between a promise and a proposal."

"I've come here night after night proving I love you. I told you what it takes to get a proposal out of me."

"Ajay is my child. I can't just throw him away."

"But you can throw me away? You can have all the boys at that government warehouse calling me a cuck because I'm getting seconds after some nigger done had you? Every time I come in here, I got to be reminded a nigger been here before me. Not a white man, but a nigger."

"What if I gave Ajay back to his daddy? He wants him."

"That ain't good enough. You can send his black ass to Africa, but some way, somehow, he's gonna pop up in my face and remind me a nigger spoiled my woman."

"Clint, the world has changed. You ought to accept..."

"Accept what? Accept niggers and wetbacks ruling over me?"

"You don't have to love 'em."

"Damn right! I ain't gonna love no nigger and I ain't gonna love no fool!"

"But Clint..."

"A new America is coming. It's going to be ten times better than the old America. In this new America, a nigger ain't going to hardly be allowed to catch dogs, much less be a goddamn president. Niggers will be glad to be slaves else they starve to death. I ain't bringing no white woman fouled by a nigger into New America. My pa, grandpa, and a half dozen other white men cleared that land for us to launch a whole 'nother America. How would I look bringing a nigger child and his ma up there?"

"His daddy can have him."

"That ain't good enough, I say."

"What do you want me to do? Kill him?"

"I want a white woman to do what she gotta do to erase that stain out of her life. I want a white woman who knows what it takes to be reborn, how to make herself ready and deserving to exist in this new world."

Jill was silent.

"You got some baby making years left in you. Let's make us a white baby. I don't want no black ghost from your past around." He nuzzled her hair and breasts. "Don't you love me?"

"Yes, Clint, I do. I do Clint. I want to do right by you."

MOTHER AND CHILD TOOK a bath together. The warm Mississippi soft water soothed Jill's nerves. She didn't mind Ajay splashing and playing with her toes. She closed her eyes and let her mind drift like debris floating down the Tallahatchie. She smelled magnolias and left solid ground. She floated above the tub. A portrait of the Madonna and Child appeared washed in blue and green lights. Her head hurt and she shut her eyes to dim the blue and greens floating in front of her eyes. Suddenly there was a banging and loud whining outside. A stench crept through the window and her head exploded in a blinding headache. When she opened her eyes, a bloody leg lay in the sand and an arm lay haphazard on the hulk of a tank. Jill saw her mother standing next to the tub before morphing into a burning cross. She found herself floating past Walmart and above the memorial marker for Emmett Till. She stood shivering in front of the carcass of the crumbling Bryant's Grocery. Blackbirds cawed overhead. A snake slithered at her feet...

"LET ME KNOW WHEN THEM faggots is coming down to collect that bastard."

"Clint just let 'em go on back to New York."

"They are going back to New York in body bags. Damned faggots. His grandpa caused us a lot of trouble way back. Somebody's got to pay for that. That old nigger Silas is half dead. But somebody is going to pay.

"Mama!"

Jill was jolted back to reality. She shivered. The bathwater had cooled, and Ajay shook her feet. She dried herself and the boy, threw on a robe, and dressed Ajay in blue Superman pajamas. The big red S blazed from his chest. She sat in her rocking chair rocking the both of them to random tunes playing through her iPod speakers. She looked at her cellphone. It was two a.m. Alvin and Bruce were due to arrive by seven. She had told Clint they wouldn't get to Money until Sunday to throw him off.

"A goddamn queer and a nigger. I can't wat to do the white race a big favor."

She could let Ajay go back with Alvin and his man friend. Clint would be mad. He wouldn't get his chance to get rid of a homo and a nigger in one fell swoop. What if Clint left because she disobeyed him? What would her life be like stuck in the projects with a black son? Maybe there was something she could do to meet Clint halfway. Maybe Alvin didn't deserve his child after all. Hadn't he used her and left her? Maybe the only memory he deserved was seeing his boy in a casket. That would serve him right—would be a just punishment for him and that man. Clint would understand. She would make him understand her wisdom. He would be appeased.

When Ajay squirmed, Jill brushed his face and whispered in his ear. He liked to rest his head on the body of the giant stuffed green dragon pillow. Jill draped the tail across the back of the chair. She rubbed Ajay's long legs and imagined he would be as tall as his father. What other characteristics would he inherit from the man who played with her feelings, Jill wondered.

"But he was just a boy," a voice whispered.

"What about me?" Jill shouted.

Ajay looked up at her. Jill cradled his face against her bosom and kissed the top of his head. She held him tight and closed her eyes. In a moment his arms began to flail, and his tiny teeth sank into her chest. "Alvin, Alvin," she whispered softly as Ajay's hands beat against her shoulders. Jill had brute strength in her good arm—strength that let had let her lift heavy Walmart pallets. Strength that let her choke the life out of her son. Mother and child rocked until the moon was high above the clouds.

IT HAD TAKEN ALVIN a bit of an effort to sell Bruce on the idea of driving down to Money Mississippi from New York with him so he could get acquainted with his son. He went ballistic when he first told him about his boy. They had gone to the city to be with his sister who had just given birth.

"Alvin, how could you keep this from me? I'm about to be your wife in a few months. You never said anything about any girl and a baby."

"I wasn't sure it was mine. She's kind of crazy."

"Not yours?" Bruce held up Alvin's baby picture his aunt had shared and compared it to the picture of Jill and Ajay. "Except for skin color, you and your child look like identical twins. How can I trust you? I believe the story about you and my best friend. I believe you did sleep with him."

Alvin and Bruce had argued all night. He stormed out of his parent's Harlem brownstone. Alvin chased after him. He took off in a cab only to come back minutes later. They yelled and screamed until they collapsed from exhaustion on opposite ends of the porch. Alvin came up with an idea but wasn't sure how to play his card. If he said the wrong thing or if his timing was off, his words might send Bruce packing for good. However, he had to try.

"Whatever I have is yours, baby. Whatever I have. Please try to understand."

Bruce froze in anger. He knew Alvin was alluding to the fact he was sterile. The idea was for them each to father a child. Bruce turned to curse him out and saw tears streaming down his face. They sat on the porch saying nothing. Harlem slowly crept to life. Another gay couple from two doors over stood on the sidewalk looking at their phones.

In a moment a car swung close to the curb. They kissed goodbye as one of them took off. Buses begin to roar past. A homeless denizen pushed a shopping cart loaded with loaves of bread across the street. Bruce's new niece began squalling. The porch light picked out a couple of strands of gray hair in Alvin's head. Bruce sighed and took his hand. They leaned together on the porch watching the sun and the moon over the Manhattan skyscrapers.

PEOPLE THREW TRASH in the murky bayou that ran behind the Medgar Evers Projects—old tires, box springs, bags of leaves. Sometimes a hunk of a car found itself moored in the muck along with dead cats and dogs. A city crew cleaned it every Monday using a garbage truck with what looked like a giant pair of claws mounted on top. It chewed through the debris and dumped the contents of the scoop into the large crusher on its back. The truck was the highlight of the day for the project's children if they were home from school.

Jill waited until the project's riffraff had gone to bed, and the moon was peeping behind clouds. Lightening lit the far-off horizon. She picked Ajay's body off the floor. His eyes stared at the ceiling. A piece of lace torn from Jill's robe, twisted through his fingers. Jill tugged at the cloth for a moment but let go. She wrapped Ajay in his favorite yellow blanket. He seemed heavy like a croaker sack of potatoes when Jill slung him over her shoulder. She opened her front door and peeped out. Her neighbor's cat that Ajay played with mewed and got up. Jill tried to shoo it away, but he rubbed her ankles, stood up on its hind legs, and sniffed at the blanket. She went back into the house and threw Ajay on the couch. She found a can of sardines in the cabinet. Jill retrieved Ajay's body, placed her cellphone in her pocket, and picked up the sardines. She ignored her prosthetic arm lying on the kitchen counter. When Jill went out the door again, the fish aroma hit the cat's nose and drove him into a frenzy. Jill put the sardines down and watched him tear into them for a moment before she headed toward the bayou. The dull light from her phone lit the grassy path. She walked barefoot with her robe tied loosely around her waist. The grass gave way to oozing mud that sucked Jill's toes. In a moment the cold water from the bayou lapped at her legs. She came to a huge tractor tire and sat down with Ajay still slung over her shoulder. Her mind traveled back to the day she found her mother dead.

When eight-year-old Jill stepped onto their trailer's porch, she stopped and sniffed. She knew if she didn't smell anything cooking that meant a supper of peanut butter sandwiches. Jill sighed and went inside. At first, when she saw her mother's bulging eyes, she thought she was playing make-believe and trying to scare her on the day before Halloween. But then Jill saw a fly light on her mother's cheek and crawl into her open mouth. A rope had been knotted around the stout ceiling fan and the other end left to make a crude noose. Her Mother's weight had bent one of the blades, and her toes were just inches from the floor. A chair lay on its side like a dead animal.

The wind rustled the trees and Jill looked up and for a moment at the branches resembling a woman's outstretched arms. "I'll never leave my child," Jill murmured to the leaves. Ajay's weight soon burdened her shoulder, and the wiry treads from the tractor tire cut into her buttocks. Jill got up and walked along the bayou until she came to a mound of trash tangled in an iron box spring. As she waded toward the middle of the bayou, water lapped at the hem of her robe and soon soaked her thighs. Ajay began to slip from her shoulders. Jill regretted she hadn't grabbed her prosthesis. She had to improvise. Jill placed Ajay on top of the spring, untied the belt of her robe and tied his body to the coils. She loosened the trash bag and set it free. With arm, Jill flipped the bedsprings over. Unbeknownst to her, part of the box spring landed on a crate so that Ajay was only partly submerged in the muddy water. The bag of trash floating down the river got caught in a tangle of twigs and branches. Curious, Jill waded toward the bag and tore it open. Baby clothes and an assortment of toys spilled out. A brown doll missing its left arm caught her eye. She clutched it to her bosom and waded back to dry land. She paused and looked back at the bayou. A log floated past and stopped, caught by the box spring. Jill turned, gathered her robe in front, and headed home. The cat, full of sardines, sat on the stairs washing his face. He stopped, looked at Jill, and continued. Once inside her apartment, she stripped out of her robe and threw it in the pile of dirty clothes on top of Ajay's Spiderman pajamas. She showered with the doll, dried off, dressed, and went outside to sweep her porch. The sun was coming up over the blue Walmart sign.

"I BROUGHT Y'ALL SOME cake and ice cream," Mamie said as she walked through the door.

"What for?"

"What for?" Mamie looked at Jill. "Ain't it Ajay's birthday?"

"Yeah," Jill answered and picked up a magazine. "But his dad came and got him."

The sheet cake nearly fell from Mamie's hands. She gazed at Jill.

"Already?"

"Yep. Came last night, him and his man friend." Jill sighed.

Mamie put the cake on the table and slung the bag of ice cream next to it. She looked around the room and noticed some of Ajay's toys scattered on the floor. Jill saw her looking.

"Flew in like a Tornado and said he wanted his boy to spend his birthday with him."

"How is he looking these days? Does he still look like a man?"

"Of course, he still looks like a man. You expect he'll turn into a frog because he's gay?"

"What this man friend look like?"

"Like a man."

"I'm sorry I missed him. Where is he staying?"

"I'm not sure."

"You're not sure?"

"Roadway Inn or Motel 8."

"You let two men walk in here and take your child, and you don't know where they're staying?"

"They'll be easy to find. It ain't like Money got a whole bunch of hotels or a bunch of gay men. And what you all worked up for? You never cared for either Alvin or Ajay that much."

"Now listen here..." Mamie stopped her lecture. She hadn't noticed the broken doll lying in Jill's lap when she walked in. She assumed Jill was sour because she missed her son. "Well, you can have the cake. I'll leave you to your moods."

"Thanks anyway," Jill said to the magazine as the screen door slammed.

ALVIN AND BRUCE DROVE into Money through the back way. It would be quicker to get to the Medgar Evers and get out. As they cut through the woods on the two-lane blacktopped road, they saw a limp confederate flag in front of a ram-shackled mobile home.

"What kind of place is this?" Bruce asked looking out the window.

"The woods were always kind of red-necked. But I never saw that before," Alvin answered.

"Hurry up, let's get through here. I hope we don't have to come this way when we leave."

"We'll take the main highway out. I want to pass by Paw Pee's old house anyway," Alvin reassured Bruce. The back seat was packed with toys—Bruce's idea. They would pick up Ajay and whisk him off to Jackson where they would spend a few days in Mississippi's largest city and figure out how to hit Jill with their proposal—total custody or joint custody—Alvin would have his son. Maybe he would see Clem if he made up and excuse to stop at Walmart. But it was Sunday. Automotive was probably closed.

As he drove, he tried to remember the ruts and turnoffs behind the trees where he went when he wanted to be alone, or to think, or to hang out with Clem. Where did he and Clem go when they wanted to fuck? Was it behind that patch of trees or those tall bushes? All he knew then was he wanted to do everything forbidden under the eyes of God and his grandfather. He imagined God watching from the sky as he and Clem carried on. He imagined his grandfather hiding up in the trees staring down sternly watching him when he was with Jill. What could God or his grandfather do? Alvin turned them into trees. Maybe shake a little, drop some leaves or small branches as trees do. But he and God could do nothing to stop him. And nothing, not even a confederate flag would stop him and Bruce.

Alvin turned in the Medgar Evers driveway and parked. He watched Bruce observe the women sitting on the stairs chatting while their children in various hues from milky tea to dark chocolate, ran around the yard playing. They had stopped just a few moments ago at the Emmett Till plaque marking the spot where the boy from Chicago had lost his life in the Tallahatchie River a few miles up.

"Hard to believe that could have happened here."

"Yeah, I guess it is." Alvin said absently. He stared at the gaggle of children to see if perhaps his son was somewhere in the mix. Bruce's eyes fell on a white woman sitting amongst the black women. Bruce looked at him.

"Nah that's not her," Alvin said. "That woman has both her arms."

The women stopped talking amongst themselves to observe the strangers looking at them. Alvin and Bruce got out of the car, and he led the way to Jill's apartment. They nodded to the women on the steps. He locked eyes with a woman in a yellow top and quickly looked off.

"Y'all going to the crazy woman's house?" A woman in a blue romper asked. Before Alvin could answer, the woman continued. "She ought to let that boy outside to play more. She and him stay cooped up in that house almost all day. She let him out sometimes to play with my cat. But that's it. Y'all from CPS?"

"I'm Ajay's father and this is my partner, Bruce."

"Lord, you that boy who used to work at Walmart. I thought you looked familiar." She turned to the woman in yellow. "Look Crystal, it's Alvin."

"I see it is," Crystal said looking at Alvin and Bruce.

"You used to come tipping around..."

Crystal elbowed the woman in blue and nodded at Bruce.

"Oh, excuse me. I'm just running off at the mouth. And you said this is...?"

"I'm Alvin's fiancé." Bruce smiled.

"Uh...oh. Who would have thought? I mean pleased to meet you." The woman grabbed Bruce's hand and held it. "I could tell you some stories. But he was different then..."

Alvin eager to get away from Crystal's steely eyes, the woman in blue, and the other gawkers, touched Bruce's elbow and guided him toward Jill's apartment. The women stared at the two men—one black and one white. The men followed a short trail of muddy footprints and stopped. Alvin tapped on Jill's door. They heard a muffled voice inside. He and Bruce hesitated.

"She in there. Go on in," the talker urged them on. All of the women except Crystal craned their necks to see inside the darkened apartment as Alvin opened the door. Once Bruce was inside, he closed the door behind him. The women shushed each other so they could hear the conversation coming from inside the apartment. The apartment was dark, but Alvin didn't want to open the curtains. He and Bruce stood for a moment before Jill turned on a table lamp.

"Hello Jill," Alvin said to the disheveled woman sitting on the couch cradling a doll. Jill looked at him and said nothing. "Um, this is my um, fiancé Bruce."

"Hello, Jill. I've heard so much about you." Bruce stuck out his hand.

"Got a whole new crew at Walmart now." Jill ignored Bruce.

"Are you still there?" Alvin asked grateful for conversation to break the ice.

"Nah. I'm on total disability."

More silence. Alvin looked at Jill and wondered how he had ever been in love with her. It couldn't have been love, he thought as he observed wisps of gray streaking through the blond mullet hairstyle. A swastika with roses was tattooed on her forearm. Her head was shaved on each side of the mullet. He knew what Bruce was saying to himself. *Really, Alvin? This is what you let ride on the back of your motorcycle? This?* The mirror showed him thicker and his face hardening into a man's face. A man ready to be responsible for his actions.

Alvin looked around the room. An assortment of toy cars and trucks littered the floor. Alvin regretted he hadn't stopped at Walmart and bought an unwrapped football or something as an offering to his son. Bruce had insisted wrapping the gifts in the back seat. He glanced toward the bedroom. Jill had gotten rid of the cot they used to romp on. In its place was a hospital bed. The table next to the bed was crammed with pill bottles. He looked at the girl doll in Jill's lap and wondered if she had had another child. If so, perhaps this new child would make it easier for her to let Ajay spend the weekend with him and Bruce. He would feel less guilty about asking Jill to let him have his son to raise. He could offer to pay her rent and a sum of cash. As he thought he became aware of the silence in the apartment.

"Um, is Ajay asleep?" Alvin asked.

"He's out playing by the river."

Bruce and Alvin looked at each other.

"By the river? By himself," Alvin asked. "The woman next door said you never let him out."

"He's out now. He's okay, dammit!"

Alvin flew out of the door and ran toward the bayou. The women on the steps looked at each other. They stood up and murmured among themselves. Inside the apartment, Jill and Bruce stared at each other.

"He's fine," Jill said. Want some cake? Yesterday was his birthday."

The women rushed to the edge of the parking lot. They watched Alvin run up and down the bayou. They saw the mud sopping up his shoes making his feet huge. He started shouting. Bruce ran to the window and looked out. The women had moved to the edge of the bayou. Some picked up sticks and steadied themselves as they walked behind Alvin. Jill sat on the couch and sighed. She picked up the doll and started to comb its hair.

"Ajay! Ajay!" Alvin shouted. The women began to yell also. Some of them raised their dresses and stepped closer to the water. They peered into the water with their hands over their chests, as if afraid of what they might see.

Alvin stopped and noticed a school of catfish in a feeding frenzy in the middle of the bayou near box springs. A buzzard landed on the banks and stared intently at the fish. A tip of the springs poked out of the muddy water. Alvin waded in, and the fish scattered as he approached. He saw a blue blanket wedged in the springs and he thought he saw, well Alvin wasn't sure what the thing was moored to the box spring. He fussed with the log lodged under the springs and set it free. By this time, Bruce had joined the women at the riverbank. They watched Alvin dip his hands into the brown water and bring up the blue blanket. A foot hung loose from one end of the cloth. At the other end was a face covered with dirt and leaves. Alvin turned and waded toward the muddy banks with the bundle in his outstretched arms as if he were keeping the muddy water away. The women screamed. A little boy started towards him until his mother caught him. Jill stood in her doorway staring at the blue Walmart sign just beyond the river. In the distance, a garbage truck rumbled down the road headed toward the Medgar Evers.

ALVIN LEANED HIS HEAD on Bruce's shoulder as the plane flew them from Jackson back to New York. Ajay rested bundled inside a metal casket inside a cardboard box. The plane ascended above the white clouds into a blueness so bright, it hurt one's eyes. "I was only eighteen. I didn't know all of this was coming," Alvin murmured. "I didn't know." Bruce held his hand.

Crystal's Letter Years Later

Dear Alvin:

Nobody hardly ever writes letters anymore. Some people barely know the alphabet these days. Just point and click on pictures. But I got thoughts in me that can only be expressed by words. I'm going to get right to the point. You had another child besides your boy Ajay. And I should have given you this other boy. You looked so pitiful holding Ajay in your arms that day. It would have been nice for my Alvee to know who his daddy was. Maybe he'd be living today. He was found murdered in that same swampy river. I didn't want to give up my child. Had no reason to. I wasn't crazy and he did all right with me until he got to be a teenager and started running with them gangs. All kind of gangs here in Money. Drug dealers and white supremacists. They got an iron fence topped with barbed wire around the Medgar Evers like it's some kind of prison. Always finding bodies in that river. Maybe I should have wrote to you and told you you had another boy and offered to send him up there to New York. Maybe I ought to have done that. Jill gave you a bitter dose of medicine. She didn't get no time for it, because they all said she was crazy. Judge wasn't going to give her no time for killing a black baby. Sent her to the insane asylum for a little while, and she was out in two years. Don't know where she went. I heard Texas. I wanted to teach you a lesson too. But I think I played a trick on myself. I might have saved Alvee's life, If I had sent him up there to you. When you was young, I wanted to give you some black girl love. You took the love like most men do and then you was gone. I wanted you so bad for myself. I wanted us to ride all the way to Atlanta on that motorcycle. We used to talk about our dreams—well I talked about mine mostly. I wanted to be a rapper like Little Kim. I don't know what you wanted to be. You didn't know either. I hear you do something with the stock market up there in New York and you and your man friend have a lot of money. I ain't wrote this letter to hurt you or ask for anything. That's not my intention even though I was hurt when you left. I guess I want to clear something up—mainly my concious. I should have told you you had another son. Should have given him to you. I had five other children by Tom, Dick, Harry, Sam, and Bob. Some of my children don't know who their daddy is. I know where some of the men are. But they are sorry men, I don't know if I ought to tell them or not. Won't make a difference. But I should have told you. I think Alvee suspected something like you and him was connected. He wanted to run up to you and wrap his arms around your legs. That's the kind of child he was. But I held him back. You had came back to town with that white man and I thought it was wrong. And I didn't want Alvee to know you was his daddy. Well Alvin, I hope somehow you got a son some kind of way. I hope the pain of that river and Jill is far away from you now. We all is heading towards old age. And I thought you ought to know. If you ever come back, you can find Alvee's grave over in Mount Olive. I got him a nice headstone. Alvee Christopher Brown. The river been through a whole lot too. One year the sun baked everything around Medgar Evers and the river got down to where it barely covered your ankles and, in some spots, as dry as the bones in it. The bottom of the river broke off into what looked like hunks of fudge and they found bones of animals and people in the Tallahatchie. Another time we got so much rain, the river swoll up and flooded all of the downstairs apartments with at least three feet of water. Snakes got inside. The river changes and you don't know what it's going to be from one year to the next. I guess you can understand that, not knowing what you're going to be from one year to the next. Well that goes for all of us. We don't know how we're going to be living from one year to the next. Money done changed too. Covid shut down almost everthing around here. Amazon delivers stuff to the few people left here. Money is falling down again, but the people is holding on the best they can.

    Love

    Crystal

About the Publisher

THE PUBLISHER AND AUTHORS from Wes Writers & Publishers[1] strive to bring you the best in fiction and poetry. We support many fine author/brands and diverse fiction genres. We strive for excellence. A better reading experience won't happen without your valuable input. That's why reviews are so helpful. Please take the time and leave a review. We also want to stay in touch with you. The best way to do so is to join our mailing list. By joining, you will get free excerpts from our upcoming titles and other important information about books and publishing. Please subscribe to the mailing list. Thank you. Subscribe[2]

CONNECT WITH HARVEY

Facebook[3]

Twitter[4]

Other Books You Will Love[5]

[6]

---

1. http://www.charlesharveyauthor.wordpress.com/

2. https://subscribepage.io/9sPXo5

3. https://www.facebook.com/pages/Wes-Writers-Publishers/200150716671422

4. https://twitter.com/CharlesHarvey99

5. https://charlesharveyauthor.wordpress.com/books/

KISS AND SAY GOODBYE[7]

6.	https://www.amazon.com/dp/B0CP4VDCWB

7. https://www.amazon.com/dp/B0CP4VDCWB

Excerpt From Kiss and Say Goodbye

Chapter 1—Playboy or Playgirl

In a moment we saw and heard the car coming, big and candy red—a Deuce-and-a-quarter with its white top glimmering under the sun. Some of us boys climbed the fence to scramble away from what was coming. Girls clutched their books, turned their faces, and squeezed their bodies to brace themselves. We were penned between Marcus Garvey's iron fence and a large puddle the size of the High school's swimming pool. The Buick came flying. The motor screamed and whined behind the car's silver sharklike grill. A wave of dirty water washed over us, stinging our faces and soaking our clothes. The car stopped and we saw the tall black boy with a bushy afro looking back grinning and gripping the steering wheel. A gaggle of cheerleaders and basketball players leaned out the Buick's windows. They hooted and pointed their middle fingers before Alphonse gunned the motor and the car whined and roared down Scott Street. It may have been me imagining things, but I thought I saw Alphonse mouthing "KK" at me in the rearview mirror.

"Alphonse! Somebody ought to kick his ass," a girl shouted into the red whirlwind fading in the distance.

The entire student body of Marcus Garvey High knew Alphonse. He always had one of his long arms wrapped around a cheerleader. Always had a girl combing and twisting his football helmet sized afro into plats. Always had his dimpled chin on a girl's shoulder. Always feeling up a girl's legs in Algebra, Biology, or English. Even in Art class when those fingers should have been holding a paint brush, or molding clay into cups and ashtrays, Alphonse's fingers teased legs when he could get away with it. If a girl protested at all, it was a weak singsong, "Stop Alphonse. Quit, boy..." which spurred him on. You could put a checkmark next to Alphonse's name for the qualities most Garvey girls considered cute—dimples, braces, slender build, thick afro with an afro pick stuck in it, wisp of a goatee and mustache, long legs faintly brushed with soft hair, long arms with slightly muscled biceps. He liked to laugh and cut up. He wore the latest threads, purple bell bottom jeans, lace shirts open to his belly button, and white Chuck Taylor tennis shoes with mismatched strings. He was the kind of boy always getting in trouble for small infractions of classroom order—making silly noises while teachers lectured, untied shoelaces, and unbuttoned shirts—always getting talked to, but never pushing things to the point of being sent to the Principal's Office to get popped.

I was as visible as the air in the room to girls, Alphonse, or any other popular kid. He brushed my shoulder when we passed in the hallways as if he was sweeping past a post. I was less than nothing in Alphonse's eyes during the period we took gym together. Well, we didn't really take gym together. Alphonse was in Coach Brown's basketball camp—a section of the gym walled off from the rusty basketball hoops and bent barbells the rest of us had to deal with. He and his teammates shot new balls through new basketball nets and dribbled over clean buffed floors while the rest of us did whatever we wanted or snoozed in the bleachers.

I kept watch over my classmates' valuables—their watches, gold chains, Polo sunglasses, and cologne. I wore a *Flexban* Timex watch. A slide rule poked out of the pocket of my too-short Kmart jeans. Kids sang *Wade in the Water* whenever I walked down the hall. My "fro" grew past the edge-up line in the back of my neck and my forehead. I looked like a poodle on a bad day or a blockhead on a good day. What's a good or bad day when you're going to be teased no matter how your hair looks? My tennis shoes looked like "Chucks," except for the big black K stamped on the sides identifying them as "Kmart specials." Kids called me KK. I dared not stretch my legs in class. I fit in by trying to blend in while Alphonse fit in by standing out. I didn't want anyone to know I paid attention to Alphonse or any boy.

Don't miss out!

Visit the website below and you can sign up to receive emails whenever Charles Harvey publishes a new book. There's no charge and no obligation.

https://books2read.com/r/B-A-EWG-NFHR

Connecting independent readers to independent writers.

Did you love *Into the Murky Water*? Then you should read *Urban Tales*[8] by Charles Harvey!

Discover the captivating world of Urban Tales, where the pulse of city life beats through the pages. These tales are a reflection of the humanity that surrounds us, a celebration of our humor, our loves, our desires, and our secret rendezvous. Only in our urban landscapes could you learn tipping over on the down-low becomes an art form.

In these stories, you'll journey through both the long and the short, the gritty and the heart-touching. Characters come alive through their elegant voices and raw urban tongues, a vibrant fusion of culture and emotion. Brace yourself for the raw truth that might stir discomfort or even bring a tear to your eye, but one thing is for certain - it will never bore you. Urban Tales are an exploration of the human experience, where

---

8. https://books2read.com/u/3yZNdl

9. https://books2read.com/u/3yZNdl

laughter and love exist alongside the poignant and profound, leaving you with thoughts that linger long after the last page is turned.

Read more at https://charlesharveyauthor.wordpress.com.

Also by Charles Harvey

Astroworld
Promise: Short Stories From The Road to Astroworld
Promise's Letters From the Road to Astroworld

Buck Wile Stories
Buck Wile is Punk'd Out On Da Downlow
Buck Wile is Butt Naked In Da City

Dogs Bark
When Dogs Bark the Short Story
Bark Too

Poetic Journeys
Americana
3AM - Poems and Stories From the Other Mind
The Last Supper
Rough Cut Until I Bleed

Roommates
Roommates and The Old Dead Seaman
Roommates and Other Stories

Standalone
Betty's House
Black Queen
The Blue Train To Heaven
The Power Plant
Ebenezer Jenkins' Christmas in Chicago
Q is a Bad Letter and Other QQ Crazy Stories
Catnip Gray Cat Detective: The Tabitha Davenport Affair
Antoine's Double Trouble
Maura And Her Two Husbands
Urban Tales
Into the Murky Water
David, Jonathan, and Sylvester
Cheeseburger and Other Stories
A Foursome Plus Poems
Kiss and Say Goodbye

Watch for more at https://charlesharveyauthor.wordpress.com.

About the Author

Charles W. Harvey is a native Houstonian and a graduate of the University of Houston. At UofH he studied fiction under the guidance of Rosellen Brown and Chitra Divakaruni. In 1987, Charles was a 1st place prize recipient of PEN/Discovery for his short story Cheeseburger, which went on to be published in the Ontario Review. In 1989 Charles Harvey was awarded the Cultural Arts Council of Houston Grant for Writers and Artists. Also in 1989 he was a finalist in the MacDonald's Literary Achievement Awards. Charles has been published in Soulfires, Story Magazine SHADE, High Infidelity, The James White Review, and others. He is the author of the novels The Butterfly Killer, The Road to Astroworld, and Antoine's Double Trouble. He is also the author of several story and poetry collections. He also writes for the stage and screen.

Read more at https://charlesharveyauthor.wordpress.com.

About the Publisher

Wes Writers and Publishers strives to bring you great books for your reading pleasure. We have been in the business of producing quality works of fiction for over two decades. We will branch out in the future to add more authors to bring you the reader, very high quality and entertaining stories from all genres. It begins with Charles W. Harvey our star prize winning literary writer an poet. He is the author of the prize winning short story Cheeseburger selected by Joyce Carol Oates in the 1987 PEN/Southwest Prize. He is a frequent participant in NANOWRIMO and other literary endeavors. Please feel free to sample his many stories and two Novels via Smashwords and other fine retailers. AC Adams brings you a little something different. He is our premier author for the gay literary erotica genre. Many of our readers have enjoyed his Roommates series. Look forward for a lot more to come from this up and coming author. Clarissa Haley comes from east Texas. She likes quirky little stories that swim around that brain of hers. She has several exciting projects in the works. She has a few romance stories in the works for future release Wes Writers and Publishers (we like being called WWP) will be adding more l writers under its wings in the near future. We love good stories.

Read more at https://charlesharveyauthor.wordpress.com.